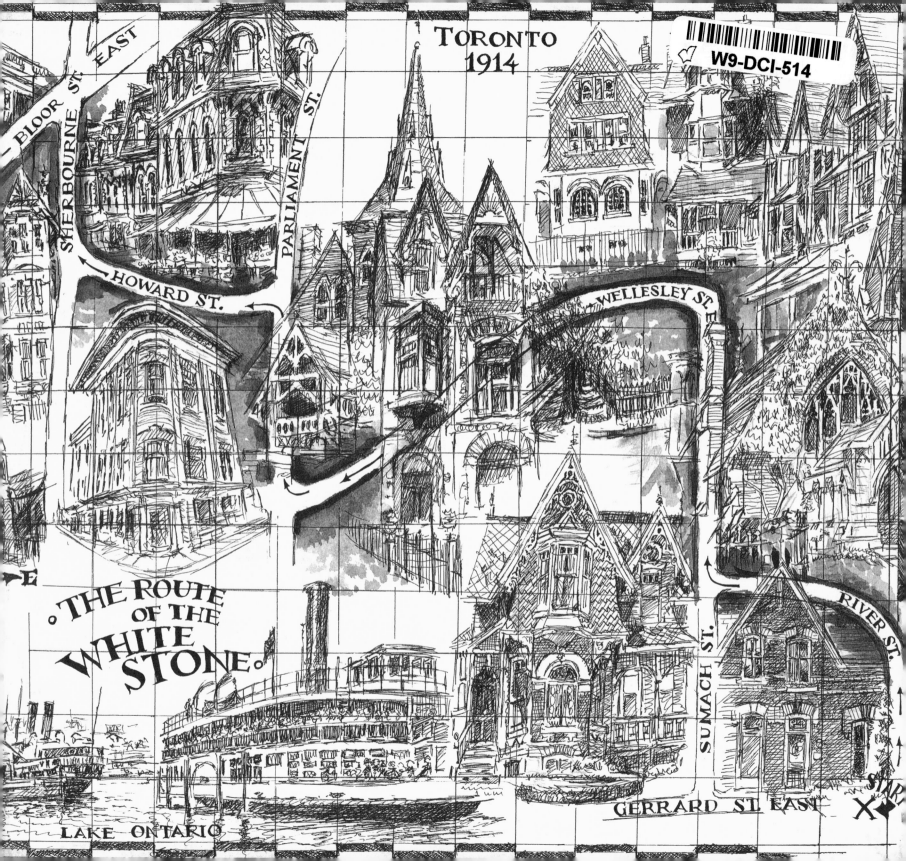

The white stone in the castle wall

story by Sheldon Oberman
paintings by Les Tait

Tundra Books

John Tommy Fiddich told everybody in his village
about his garden where he worked hard every day.

"I grow tomatoes and cabbages, potatoes and radishes, pumpkins and lots of green beans. I will sell them in the market and earn a silver dollar. I am the luckiest boy of all."

Then the hail beat everything down,
the insects ate everything up,
and the wind blew the rest away
except for a dirty, gray stone.

John Tommy Fiddich told everybody in his village:
      "My garden is totally destroyed.
      I have no tomatoes or cabbages, no potatoes or radishes,
      no pumpkins or a single green bean.
      All I have left is this dirty, worthless stone.
      It sticks in the ground and it gets in the way.
      It's cold and rough for a place to sit
      and nothing can grow over it
      and nothing can get under it
      and it's far too hard to even kick.
      I am the unluckiest boy of all."

Then came news from Sir Henry M. Pellatt
who owned all the lights in the streets of the city,
who owned Casa Loma, the great castle on the hill.

He was building a wall around Casa Loma.
He wanted big stones that were colored dull black,
dull red or brown, dull green or gray.
He would pay a silver dollar for each one.

John pushed and he pulled. He lifted and shoved.
He rolled his stone into a cart.
He said:
>"I'll get a dollar for this dirty, worthless stone.
>I am the luckiest boy of all."

Some people hauled their stones from the country with a tractor.
Some people brought their stones to the city on a train.
Some towed them on a barge that floated through canal ways.
Some shipped their stones across the lake on boats with canvas sails.

Then all the stones were lifted and loaded onto wagons
and everyone went racing to the castle on the hill.

John had
to work
far harder
than
them.

He had
to pull
and
to push
and
to shove.

But his stone
was
so heavy
and
his cart
was
so old
that
they all
passed him by
in a rush.

Soon the clouds began to gather,
the sky began to darken,
the wind rose and the rain
fell hard and fast.

John kept pulling onward
looking forward,
never backward,
not seeing
what the rain did
to his stone,
not seeing
all its gray dirt
wash away.

John reached the muddy hilltop and he waited there for hours

until finally his turn came to sell his stone.

The master of the wall looked closely at the stone.

He shook his head. He turned to John and said:
    "Sir Henry M. Pellatt called for dull-colored stones:
    dull black, dull red or brown, dull green or gray.
    Your stone is all bright white. Sir Pellatt will not want it.
    I cannot buy it from you for his wall."

John said:
    "But Sir Henry owns this great castle.
    He owns all the lights in the streets of the city.
    All that I own is this one white stone
    and I hauled it up the hill for him."

The builders of the wall,
the drivers of the wagons,
the servants of the castle all said:
    "John Tommy Fiddich, your white stone is worthless.
    You're the unluckiest boy of all."

John left them and he rested
in the garden of the castle,
full of fountains and flowers and birds.

There he saw a man who whistled
as he planted young red roses,
and hummed as he pulled out
all the weeds.

John told him:
      "I once grew a vegetable garden
      but the only thing it gave me
      was this stone.
      I'm too tired to return it.
      You can have it
      if you'll use it.
      I just don't want to see it
      thrown away."

The man asked John:
    "Why do you care about a stone?"

John answered:
    "At first, I thought it was a worthless thing
    until I dug it up and pushed it up
    and hauled it to the hilltop
    and stood with it for hours in the mud.
    Now I'm tired, wet and hungry
    and this stone won't fetch a penny
    but my work has made it worth a lot to me."

"My name," said the man, "is Sir Henry M. Pellatt
    and I've cared for my garden just like you.
    I will buy your great white stone
    and I will put it in my wall
    because your work has made it worth a lot to me."

Sir Henry showed John through
every part of his great castle.
He let John ride in his electric car.
Then he gave John Tommy Fiddich a shining silver dollar.
And he said:
    "Please come and help me in my English flower garden.
    You will like the work and I will pay you well."

The workers at the castle,
the visitors to the garden,
everybody in the village,
all said:

"John Tommy Fiddich,
you have a job at Casa Loma.
You're the luckiest boy of all."

"I've been lucky
and unlucky,"
said John Tommy Fiddich.

"But I've earned a silver dollar
all the same.
And I brought Sir Henry Pellatt
a great white stone
for Casa Loma,
a stone that's worth a lot
to him
and to me."

Sir Henry Pellatt was a spectacular individual and the spectacular castle he built is a fitting monument to his dreams and achievements — and to his generosity.

He was born in Kingston, Ontario in 1859, and the family moved to Toronto the following year. He was such a good athlete that at age 20 he won the amateur championship of America for the mile running race. The following year he joined the Queen's Own Rifles and by the end of World War I he was a brigadier-general.

Generous to his fellow soldiers — as he would later be to his employees—he took the bugle band of his regiment to England at his own expense in 1902 to attend the coronation of King Edward VII. He was knighted by that same king in 1905.

As a businessman, he was open to new ideas in a Canada that was opening up to the West and the North, and he invested successfully in railways and mines. The business venture he is best known for was harnessing the power of Niagara Falls to bring electricity to the city of Toronto. He also introduced the first electric automobile and electric streetcars.

Stories of his eccentricity continue to delight: when his favorite horse, Prince, lost his teeth, Sir Henry replaced them with dentures. His particular love was his English garden which he liked to tend, dressed like a workman.

By 1910, he was worth $17 million, which made him one of the richest men in Canada at the time, and the following year he started to build Casa Loma, the castle that remains his memorable achievement.

Casa Loma, meaning house on the hill, took 300 workers three years to build. It had 98 rooms, 21 marble fireplaces, 30 bathrooms (some with taps that ran perfumed water) and the city's first electric elevator. The kitchens had three ovens, each large enough to roast an ox. The furnace was big enough to power the *Titanic*. There was a shooting gallery, a refrigerated wine cellar for 1,800 bottles, two bowling alleys and — in keeping with its medieval structure — two secret passages.

When the time came to build a wall around the castle, in an act of flamboyant generosity he announced that he would buy fieldstones from ordinary citizens and pay a dollar for each stone (a phenomenal sum since that was the wage of a skilled worker for an eleven-hour day). The 250,000 stones needed to build the half-mile of walls around the castle were purchased by his foreman according to strict specifications under Sir Henry's personal supervision.

So how did that one white stone get into the wall? It could only have been with Sir Henry's approval.

Eighty years ago Toronto was a city whose population had almost doubled in the preceding decade. Poor families crowded into one or two rooms for shelter; even stables were used. The poorest squatted on unused land in shacks and tents on Poplar Road down the hill from Casa Loma.

John Tommy Fiddich would have lived closer to Lake Ontario in the Cabbagetown section of Toronto. Many of the buildings in the illustrations can still be seen by anyone following his route up the hill, pushing that stone. The white stone itself is in the wall just to the right of the lower gate on Davenport Road.

Dedications

Two days after I wrote this story, I met a young boy named Sam Peden. He was carrying home a large and heavy stone that he had found in the woods. I was amazed because Sam was acting so much like John Tommy Fiddich and his stone was made of the same white quartz as the white stone of Casa Loma. I dedicate this book to Sam. — Sheldon Oberman

I would like to dedicate the paintings in this book to my wife Nancy, my daughter Madeleine and my son Sam because they helped me push that white stone all the way up the hill. — Les Tait

---

© **1995 Sheldon Oberman: text**
© **1995 Les Tait: art**

Published in Canada by Tundra Books, Montreal, Quebec H3Z 2N2

Published in the United States by Tundra Books of Northern New York, Plattsburgh, N.Y. 12901

Library of Congress Catalog Number: 95-60978

Canadian Cataloging in Publication Data:
Oberman, Sheldon
  The white stone in the castle wall
ISBN 0-88776-333-2 (hardcover) 10 9 8 7 6 5 4 3 2 1
  1. Casa Loma (Toronto, Ont.) — Juvenile fiction.
I. Tait, Les, 1949- . II. Title.

PS8579.B47W44 1995   jC813'.54   C94-900045-0 P27.034Wh 1995

Design by Dan O'Leary

Transparencies by Michel Filion

Printed in Hong Kong by South China Printing Co. Ltd.